Go Go Gorillas

A Romping Bedtime Tale

Written by **Patrick Wensink**   Illustrated by **Nate Wragg**

SCHOLASTIC INC.

For Walter and Leah
—P.W.

For Willow, my little party animal
—N.W.

ISBN 978-1-338-56382-5

Text copyright © 2017 by Patrick Wensink. Illustrations copyright © 2017 by Nate Wragg.
All rights reserved. Published by Scholastic Inc., 557 Broadway, New York, NY 10012,
by arrangement with HarperCollins Children's Books, a division of HarperCollins Publishers.
SCHOLASTIC and associated logos are trademarks and/or registered trademarks of Scholastic Inc.

12 11 10 9 8 7 6 5 4 3 2 1   19 20 21 22 23 24

Printed in the U.S.A.   40

This edition first printing, January 2019

The artist used acrylic paints and digital color to create the digital illustrations for this book.
Typography by Dana Fritts

On every safari, gorillas come last.
Most kids never stop—they just speed right on past.

Gorillas

They claim apes are dull. They say, "Apes are boring!"
"This one is yawning! And this one is snoring!"

But they're not as lazy as everyone thinks.
These apes have a reason they need forty winks.

Wait until dark, when they think you can't see.
That's when our apes get footloose and free.

It's the end of the day, so a giant meal's first.
They chomp so much food that their bellies could burst.

Bananas in bunches all vanish like ghosts.
Mountains of marshmallows sit ready to toast.

Then Jungle Jed comes, and he speaks soft and low.
"All you apes grab your jammies. Go, go, go, go.

"Brush your teeth, comb your fur, read a story or two.
In the morning, more people will be here for you!"

For a minute or more, it might look like they're sleeping.
But soon they're unleashing the secret they're keeping.

Slowly and slyly, each slips from a bunk.
Baby picks records of reggae and funk.

This trend catches on as their toes give a wiggle.
Their arms loosen up and their hips start to jiggle.
Now, this is a party! The night of all nights!
Mirror balls, DJs, and bright flashing lights.

The dance floor goes crazy—the apes form a ring,
all swirling and twirling and strutting to swing.

Some tango, some Charleston, one does the fox-trot.

But Baby is old school: he does the robot!

The fun's really roaring—then Jed's at the door.
Apes fall from the ceiling and land on the floor.

"It's bedtime!" he shouts. "And here's my last warning.
You know all the children will be here by morning."

The apes hush themselves. Soon they're all zonked out cold.
You can hear great big snores from the young and the old.

Look at how cute—the apes are all dreaming.
Jed's proud of himself. He walks away, beaming.

Hey . . .
WAIT A MINUTE. . . .

From the waltz to the polka, apes know every dance.
Each time the clock chimes, they all conga like ants.

It's the time of their lives! Some swing from treetops!
Then Jed storms back in—and the whole room just stops.

They hold in their breath while Jed shakes his big fist.
That shake spreads through his body. "Let's all do the twist!"

Jed chooses a partner. He calls out a tune.
No wonder they love dancing under the moon!

Jed wows the whole crowd with his feet oh so light,
and they groove and they boogie away the whole night.

The secret dance ends as the sunlight starts dawning.
The apes move so slowly. They're stretching and yawning.
This trouble is double for one jungle guide—
Jed grabs a big blanket, crawls under to hide.

See, you can't blame gorillas for snoozing all day.
They just don't have pep left for smiling and play.

Think twice if you're tempted to pass them on by. . . .

Tonight they might need a dance partner your size!